The Demon's Curvy Angel: A Halloween Romance

Holiday Romance, Volume 1

Brill Harper

Published by Brill Harper, 2023.

This is a work of fiction. Similarities to real people, places, or events are entirely coincidental.

THE DEMON'S CURVY ANGEL: A HALLOWEEN ROMANCE

First edition. October 16, 2023.

ISBN: 979-8223515562

Written by Brill Harper.

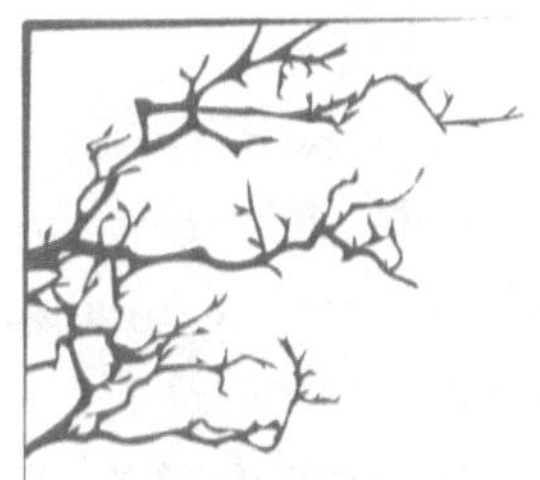

One
Maribelle

The bar throbs with the beat of the music, a heavy bass that thrums in time with my racing pulse. My friends chatter and laugh around me, a tray of shot glasses between us. We've got slutty nurse, slutty witch, slutty French maid, and me. Not slutty angel.

"Nurse" Gia offers me a shot glass. "C'mon. Celebrate. It's Halloween."

"I don't want a hangover tomorrow."

My new job starts Monday, and I want Sunday to prepare. Pick out my outfits, get groceries for the week, stress out...the usual.

My gaze wanders the room, skipping past goblins and ghosts until it lands on a figure in the corner. Black leather stretches across broad shoulders and down muscled arms. A pair of small horns jut from a mess of ebony hair, and when he turns, his eyes glow red in the shadows.

Heat floods my cheeks. I press my thighs together, acutely aware of the ache building between them. My heart just *stutters* at the sight of him, this demon stalking the edges of the room. Watching. Waiting.

Hungry.

His gaze finds mine from across the bar, and a slow smile spreads across his face, revealing the glint of sharp teeth. The bass line of the music seems to fade, the shouts and laughter of the crowd dimming until there is only him, this creature of sin and temptation gazing at me with eyes glowing like embers.

I lick my lips, and his smile widens. He begins moving through the crowd, the sea of revelers parting before him. Each step brings him closer.

Closer.

The ache between my legs grows, an emptiness I've never known and one only he can fill. My heart races as he approaches, each beat a staccato rhythm of need, desire, lust.

I have only one thought as he stalks toward me. A single word echoes in my mind, drowning out all else.

Yes.

Gia nudges me. "Shit. Mark is here."

Her words cut through the haze of desire like a scratching record, and I jerk my gaze away from the *demon's* smoldering eyes.

My ex, Mark, stands a few feet away from our table, his arm draped over the shoulders of his girlfriend, Tiffany. She gives me a smug little wave, her diamond engagement ring winking under the strobe lights.

Rage and humiliation rise in my chest. Mark hates this bar. He's only here to taunt me some more. I lift my chin, refusing to give him the satisfaction.

Why is he dragging this out? We broke up six months ago so he could be with Tiffany. Why won't he just go away now?

"Happy Halloween, Maribelle." Mark's voice is almost defensive, and I can feel Tiffany's eyes on me. "Didn't expect to see you here."

Right. I smile tightly, my hands clenching at my sides. "I could say the same to you."

Because you hate this bar.

Mark shrugs, taking a sip of his beer. "Tiffany wanted to come."

It's then I take in their costumes. Tiffany is a sexy bunny, and Mark, wearing silk pajamas, is apparently Hefner. I roll my eyes. She's fine, but I have issues with any man emulating that man, but most especially one I used to date. Gross.

"It's been great catching up, Mark, but I don't want to keep you," I say. It's been anything but great. He wanted me to see his skinny girlfriend wearing his ring. Mission accomplished.

I suppose it's supposed to punctuate that I'm *still* single and *still* chubby. As far as I'm concerned, this is how I am happy to stay.

Mark nods at my friends. "I see you're still attached at the hip to your girl gang."

Like it's a problem if I have friends?

"She's here with someone tonight," drunk nurse Gia helpfully replies.

"Right," Mark says. "Sure she is."

Hey, I could be here with someone. I'm not but I could be. I don't really want to find a fake date to save face, though.

I clench my hands into fists, my nails biting into my palms. I won't give him the satisfaction of a reaction. I won't—

"I've been looking for you everywhere, angel." The voice is a silken purr, and a hand settles on the small of my back with a possessive warmth that spreads through my body.

It's my demon man. I know without looking.

My girl gang gasps.

The devil turns me into his muscled arms and flattens me to his broad chest. His mouth crashes into mine, and I moan as his tongue slides into my mouth.

Okay, stranger tongue in my mouth. This is not something I am normally okay with, but I will make an exception for the *hottest man I have ever seen*. Or smelled. My God, he's delicious.

I wrap my arms around his neck, pulling him even closer. The hard length of him presses against me, and my body responds eagerly. I've been waiting my whole life to be kissed like this.

Mark coughs awkwardly, and my own personal demon pulls away, sizing Mark up in a way that makes it very clear who the alpha male is in this situation. Mark looks away first, submissive to the powerful presence of my rescuer.

It's a moment I'll savor forever.

Satan = 1; Cheating Bastard = 0

"Whatever," Mark mutters, grabbing Tiffany's hand. He stalks away without another word, but not before I glimpse the unease in his eyes.

"Thank you," I say softly, tilting my head back to meet the demon's gaze. His eyes glow like embers in the dim light, seeing into the darkest parts of my soul.

Those are some amazing contact lenses.

Up close, I see he's painted a tattoo of swirling black on one side of his face. An interesting choice, not one I've seen on demon costumes before. This guy is next-level devil.

"You're welcome, little angel." His smile is slow and sinful, a promise of wicked delights to come. "Now, I believe you owe me a dance."

My girl gang sighs.

I take his hand without hesitation, letting him lead me onto the dance floor. The music pulses around us, primal and seductive, as he pulls me close to him. He towers over me, indeed making me feel petite. His little angel.

His hands settle on my waist, scorching brands that ignite my skin even through the layers of my costume. I place my hands on his shoulders, acutely aware of the firm muscle beneath.

We move together effortlessly, our bodies finding a rhythm as if we've danced this way countless times. He dips his head, lips brushing the shell of my ear, and a full-body shiver wracks me.

"What's your name, little angel?" he asks, his voice a husky caress.

"Maribelle." I cling to him as the song changes, the beat turning wild and frenetic.

A secretive smile plays about his lips. "I'm Lucrael."

The name rolls off his tongue like a sin, as dark and enticing as the man himself.

"Lucrael." I taste the word on my lips, savoring the way it feels to speak it.

His eyes flash at the sound, hands tightening on my waist to pull me impossibly closer. I go willingly, drowning in the heat and scent of him, of leather and spice with an undertone of smoke.

The song ends but he doesn't release me, leaning down to slant his mouth over mine. I melt into the kiss, clinging to him as a raging inferno consumes me from within, burning away any lingering doubts or fears.

"Come home with me," I say.

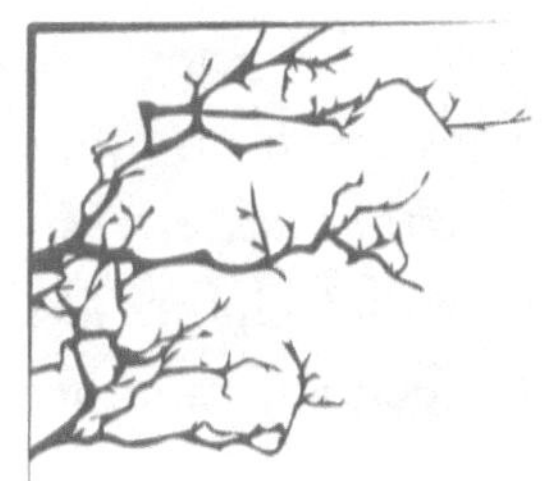

Two
Maribelle

I am not the girl to take strangers home with me. I'm not even drunk. I don't know what has come over me. But I know what I want to come over me.

All over me.

Maybe it's the thrill of the moment, the dangerous allure of the "demon" in front of me. But before I can take the invitation back, Lucrael's lips curve into a wicked smile.

"I thought you'd never ask," he says, his hand slipping into mine as we make our way to the door past my girl gang, each staring at me with wide eyes. Past scowling Mark and jealous Tiffany.

How's that ring feel now, Tiff?

Outside, the night air is cool and crisp, a welcome relief from the heat of the club. I'm surprised to find Lucrael has a car and driver waiting for us out front.

So my demon savior is rich, too. It's possible that this is a dream. I hope I don't wake up before the orgasm. I haven't had a really good one in a long time.

Lucrael's hand rests on my thigh, his touch sending sparks throughout my body. I can't believe I'm doing this, but at the same time, I can't imagine stopping.

Though I am buckled in securely, Lucrael is not. He surrounds me in his heat as his mouth comes down on mine, claiming me in a fierce kiss and pressing me into the backrest. His hands roam over my body, groping me through my clothes like he can't stop himself. The restraint of the seat belt adds another layer of excitement to the situation, frankly.

I'm trapped.

At the mercy of a demon.

I feel his impressive arousal pressing against me, and I grind my hips against him, seeking more friction. I don't care what the driver thinks. Maybe he's used to it. Maybe this happens three times a week.

I should care, but I don't.

The car ride is a blur of lust and desire, Lucrael's hands and mouth never leaving my body.

We stumble into my apartment, a tangle of lips and limbs. By the time we reach my bedroom, I am completely divested of all traces of angel, as naked as Eve before the unfortunate apple business. Lucrael still wears his boxer briefs and horns.

He's gorgeous, all hard muscle and sinew. But it's his eyes that captivate me, glowing with an unearthly light, bright embers in the shadows. I shiver at the intensity of his gaze, feeling exposed, laid bare.

This is the part where I start worrying about my extra pudge. I mean, he's here in my bedroom, so it must not bother him. I wasn't wearing any shaping underwear or anything to conceal my body type, so he must be into it. Some men prefer the cushion. But it's hard not to feel self-conscious with a veritable god in your bedroom, you know? Especially after the parting words in my bad breakup included the phrase "too fat."

Before I go down that road too far, I am pushed against the wall and Lucrael is devouring my neck and my chest with his hot mouth.

"So beautiful," he rasps, reaching out to trace the curve of my stomach, caressing it with adoration. "My angel."

I lean into his caress with a soft sigh. "Yours."

A growl rumbles in his chest at my surrender. He cages me against the wall, one hand braced beside my head while the other cups my breast, rolling the nipple between his fingers. I whimper at the sensation, desire coiling tight within me.

"Say it again." His voice is rough with barely leashed need. Commanding.

"I'm yours," I breathe.

He claims my mouth in a searing kiss, all tongue and sinful pleasure. I cling to him, consumed by the inferno raging inside me, burning away any lingering doubts about giving myself over to this stranger.

We tumble onto the bed and he rises over me, braced on his forearms. His eyes glow brighter now, twin flames in the darkness, and when he smiles I glimpse the hint of fangs behind his lips.

When I look again, the fangs are gone. A trick of the light perhaps. I stare up at him, trembling with a mix of fear and longing. It's easy to get caught up in the Halloween vibes and let my imagination run wild. I want to believe he's something more than human, something mystical and powerful.

My dark prince.

His hand slides between us, his fingers caressing my sensitive flesh. I gasp, arching into his touch. He smiles, a wicked grin that sets my heart racing. He knows he has me, and he's enjoying it.

"So wet for me," he purrs, his voice a low rumble. "I must taste this perfect pussy."

I moan in pleasure as he slides his fingers into my slick heat, exploring and teasing me. His tongue traces a line from my navel to my clit, licking and nibbling my skin until I'm squirming beneath him, desperate for more.

"Hold onto my horns," he growls.

I wrap my hands around the ridges, my fingers tingling at the contact. He shudders at my touch, as if the devil horns are really a part of him.

What kind of costume is this?

And then I no longer care.

His tongue seems longer now, more serpentine, and he licks at my clit causing a pleasure that borders on pain it's so intense. My body pulses, sensations rippling through me like waves in an ocean. Then he enters me with that tongue.

Holy hell.

He's using it like a cock. It feels as if his tongue is forked or something. The tip moves separately from his deep thrusts, tickling my inner walls. I let out a loud moan and he chuckles, the vibrations of his laughter sending me even closer to the edge.

I've never been fucked with a tongue before. It's savage and dirty and wonderful. Mark used to give me a few cursory licks now and then, but Lucrael uses his tongue as if it's the main event. His growls and groans let me know he's enjoying it too, and his fingers grip my hips, anchoring me in place as he ravishes me.

My climax builds until I'm sure I'm about to burst. I press my hips against him, my body desperate for more. He responds with a flurry of thrusts, pushing me closer and closer to the edge until I'm crying out his name.

When he pulls away, all I can see is glowing eyes and horns.

He's not wearing a costume. He is the costume.

He is the darkness.

"Such a good girl," he purrs. "Sleep now, angel."

My eyes close as commanded, and sleep overtakes me.

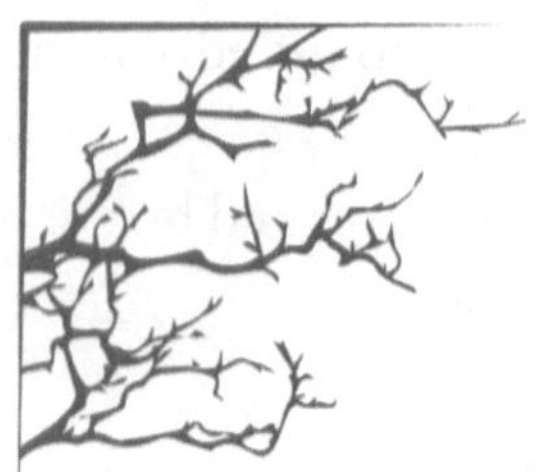

Three
Maribelle

The early morning light wakes me from a deep slumber. I reach across the rumpled sheets. But my hand finds only empty space.

Disappointment wells in my chest. Of course he's gone. A man like that would never linger until morning, not for a mousy thing like me. I'm not the type men pine for. How I even grabbed his attention last night is a mystery.

Maybe he thought it was hot to fuck an angel in white when he was dressed like a demon.

It was hot.

But we didn't actually fuck. Well, except with his tongue.

The memory causes a sudden flush of heat to flood my cheeks. I can still *feel* his tongue inside me, still feel the pleasure that came with it.

But my demon lover never even got all the way naked. Which is a shame.

He didn't even come. Which is another shame.

With a sigh, I drag myself from the lonely bed and shuffle to the bathroom. My reflection stares back at me, as ordinary as ever. My messy brown hair and tired eyes hold no allure or mystery. Lucrael probably forgot me the moment he walked out the door.

I turn the shower on hot, letting the steam cloud the mirror. As I step under the scalding spray, I try to hold onto the memories of last night - the brush of his fingers over my skin, the heat in his gaze, that magic tongue. But the details are already fading.

By the time I've toweled off and dressed, I've steeled myself against false hope. Whatever happened between us was merely a Halloween fancy, as temporary as our costumes. Best to tuck it away like an old photograph, a glimpse of a world too perfect to be real.

I have to focus on the present now. My new job starts tomorrow. I have things to do.

Gia texts me. "I require proof of life."

I snap a selfie back to her.

"Is he still there?"

"No."

My phone rings and my heart speeds up. I didn't give him my number, but maybe...

GIA CALLING

Stupid false hope. I guess I didn't steel myself as well as I thought.

I swipe to answer, determined not to get wrapped up in an obvious one-night stand.

"Tell me everything," Gia says. "Do not leave one single detail out. God that was so cool how he swooped in and made Mark look like a tool. I mean, Mark is a tool so it's not that hard. But damn, Maribelle. That demon was *fine*."

"Yes, he was," I agree.

"Okay, spill. Tell me everything."

I tell Gia...*most* things. And then I do my errands and water my plants and try to forget the hottest night of my life.

Gathering my costume together from the floor, I realize I have lost my halo.

ON MONDAY MORNING, the office of Blackstone Enterprises is already a hive of activity when I arrive, people bustling about with armfuls of documents.

The receptionist has the largest to-go cup of coffee I have ever seen sitting on her desk. She sees me staring at it. "Still recovering from Halloween," she explains.

"I feel that."

"I think I got turned into a zombie. I've never had a hangover last this long."

"You look really good for a zombie."

She smiles. "How can I help you, new best friend?"

"I'm Maribelle Saunders, the new assistant to Evelyn James. I start today, but I don't know where to go."

"Of course. I'll let her know you are here. You're going to love working for her. Ms. James is very, very smart. And sweet, unless you get on her bad side. She's very protective of Mr. Blackstone. Nobody gets to him without going through her first."

Ms. James is about ninety pounds soaking wet, but I can see how getting through her would be no easy task. She is the administrative assistant to Mr. Blackstone, the CEO, and I am her assistant. Which makes me the assistant to the assistant, I guess.

Ms. James shows me my desk and then tours me around the office. At noon, she sends me out for Mr. Blackstone's lunch, instructing me to bring it to his office as she will be out of the building for a few hours.

I use the intercom on her desk to ring his office when I get back.

"Yes?"

"Ms. James asked me to bring you lunch, sir? I'm her new assistant."

"Enter."

I don't know why I'm so nervous. Everyone in the break room told me he's a fair man who expects a lot, but compensates well and is the best boss they've had. He always lays out his expectations clearly, they said.

I enter the personal office, not knowing what to expect, but sort of assuming an older man with silver hair. Maybe glasses and a paunch. Ms. James is probably in her sixties, so he's probably a few years older than her. I don't know how long they worked together, so–

What the actual fuck?

Instead of a silver-haired paunchy father figure, I'm confronted with a tall, devilishly handsome man in his mid-thirties, with a shock of dark hair that falls just over his forehead. A man who wears a suit that looks like it costs more than my monthly rent. A man who bears a striking resemblance to my one-night stand.

Right down to the horns on his head and the face tattoo.

He recovers from his shock faster than I do.

"This is a surprise," he says smoothly.

Surprise. Yes. "How...why...am I dreaming this right now?"

He laughs, a low sound that vibrates through my bones. "No, you're not dreaming." He gets up from his desk. "This is awkward, I'm afraid. I'm Luc Blackstone, CEO of Blackstone Enterprises."

"You recognize me though, right?"

"Of course, I do. You're a hard woman to forget, angel. Is that my lunch?"

My head is spinning, but I manage to nod. Power radiates from him. Our eyes meet, and an electric current passes between us. "You told me your name was Lucrael."

"Most people call me Luc. But you're not most people, are you?" He frowns. "Are you all right, Maribelle? Perhaps you should sit down."

I'm not all right. Not all right at all. I had a one-night stand with my boss's boss. Now I'm probably going to lose this job. And there is also no chance that anything more will ever happen with him again because...boss's boss. Not that I really thought it would. But the *hope* of a cool drink of water felt nice after the six-month drought post breaking up with Mark.

I let my soon-to-be ex-boss guide me to the chair opposite his desk. I sit, and he takes the lunch bag from my hands.

"I'm sorry," I whisper. "I don't usually have...with strangers..I..."

"Don't apologize," he says. "It was a memorable night. No regrets."

My face flames. "But you're my boss."

"I didn't know you were an employee. Evelyn doesn't need to clear her hires with me, so I never saw your file. I'm assuming from the shock on your face you didn't know I was your employer. Now we know." He holds his hands out. "No harm done."

I take a deep breath and try to process my thoughts. He's right. No harm done.

Still employed, but also still single.

"Thank you," I say, finally. "I appreciate your understanding."

"We'll need to keep Halloween between us, of course."

"Of course."

"And I'm afraid it can't happen again." He sounds regretful, but then again, he didn't leave me his number when he spirited out of my bed in the early morning hours either.

He sits behind his desk and opens the bag as if everything is back to normal now. As if he hasn't turned my life upside down several times since I saw him across the bar Saturday night.

I need to get out of here. "If there's nothing else Lu...Mr. Blackstone?"

He shakes his head. Again, he looks regretful.

I take two steps to the door when I remember what else is strange. The fact that I momentarily forgot is a testament to how weird this day has become. I turn. "Mr. Blackstone? May I ask why you are still wearing your costume?"

"What do you mean, Maribelle?

I hold my fingers up to my head to mimic horns. Maybe he forgot to remove them and everyone else has been too afraid to bring it up. But, how are they even affixed to his head? I pulled them pretty hard the other night, and they didn't budge.

Lucrael rises from his desk and prowls towards me. I fight the urge to back away, standing my ground. He circles me slowly, and I feel his gaze drag over every inch of my body.

"Tell me," he murmurs, his voice darker, thicker, "how is it that you can see what others cannot?"

My pulse kicks up a notch. "What do you mean?"

His fingers graze my neck, raising goosebumps. "My true form," he purrs. "Humans can't see my true form."

I shiver at his touch. "I-I don't know what you mean." Suddenly, his hand closes around my wrist. "I think you do," he growls. "What are you if you're not human?"

Well, doesn't it just figure. I have the best sex that wasn't sex of my life, and my lover turns out to be a nut job. "I'm human, sir. If you just let go of my wrist, I'll get out of your hair."

And flee the office. And, shit, I should probably move since he knows where I live. I'm guessing this is one of those teachable moments about taking strangers home from bars.

"You smell human."

Okay, then. Now he's sniffing me. "I am, sir."

If I can just get back into the outer office, I'll be fine. There are lots of people out there. Lots of witnesses.

Though you'd think at least one person in that break room could have mentioned the fair boss who compensates well also cosplays that he's the devil 24/7. It really should have come up.

"I'd given up hope of ever finding you," he says.

The office walls vanish around us, replaced by a luxurious living room with floor-to-ceiling windows overlooking the city from high above.

"What?" I start to slide to the floor, but Lucrael catches me. "What just happened? Where are we?"

"My penthouse. This conversation requires complete privacy."

I turn to face him. "How did we get here?"

"Do you really not know? You're not a supernatural? You really are a human?"

"Mr. Blackstone, I am a human. I swear. Please stop asking me that. Did you drug me? How did you get me past all the employees? Do you have some secret trap door in your office?"

"I'm a demon, Maribelle. I used magic to bring us here."

Thud. Thud. Thud goes my heart. That is the most ridiculous thing I've ever heard. He can't be a demon. Demons don't exist. And if he can just magic me places, why did we spend that interminable car ride to my apartment after we left the club?

No. He must have drugged me and put me in a dumb waiter or laundry shoot that goes from his office to the parking garage, then somehow convinced his driver to take us here without calling the police.

"You don't believe me," he says simply.

I gape at my new surroundings. A penthouse he somehow magicked me to. Right.

"This is real, Maribelle."

"Um, okay."

I don't feel drugged. I've watched enough true crime docs to know that waking up after a roofie or chloroformed rag is supposed to be unpleasant. I'm shaky, but not nauseous. My head feels fine. I'm confused but not disoriented.

But if he didn't drug me, then he's a demon.

His horns weren't bought at a fancy costume store. He's not wearing contact lenses. That tattoo on his face is not makeup.

Lucrael Blackstone is a real demon. A real demon who is very large, very handsome, and very intensely staring at me right now.

Fear and desire war within me. What have I gotten myself into? And why does part of me thrill at the darkness awaiting me here?

I meet his burning gaze. "What happens now?"

A slow, wicked smile spreads across his face, revealing a hint of fang. "Now, my little angel, the real fun begins."

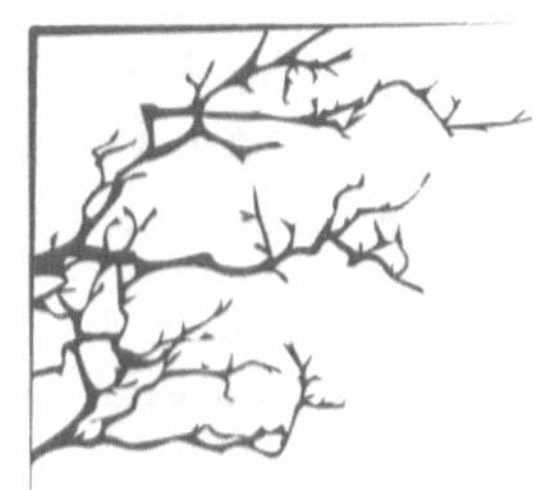

Four
Lucrael

Need simmers in my veins, an ache that threatens to consume me whole. My true mate. After centuries of searching, she is finally within my grasp.

Maribelle stands before me, arms crossed over her chest. Her eyes betray the nerves fluttering in her stomach. She has no idea what I have planned for her now that I have finally found her.

She will be the most satisfied woman on the planet. In all the realms. I shall make her come uncontrollably, over and over again, until she can barely even remember her own name.

I step closer to her, my eyes drinking in every inch of her body. She is even more perfect than I remember. Her curves are exquisite. My cock is stirring in my pants, aching to be inside her.

Maribelle's eyes widen as she realizes what I want from her. Her lips part, as if to protest, but I know that deep down she wants this as much as I do.

"What do you mean by fun?" Her scent intoxicates me. "What is going on?"

I should have known on Halloween that she was the one. The intoxicating way she tasted when she came on my tongue, the way I've thought of nothing but her since I left her apartment...apparently, my loss of faith in ever finding my bride blinded me to what was in plain sight.

I drink in each tremble of her pulse. "You are special, Maribelle. Unique." My hands find her waist, squeezing as I pull her flush against me. "You are the only one who can give me what I crave most."

Her breath hitches, eyes widening. "What are you talking about?"

"Children." The word is a growl, rumbling from my chest. My cock strains against my trousers at the thought of filling her, breeding her. "You are my destined mate. The prophecy foretold that only one human woman could bear my young and break my curse. The one who could see my true form. You are the only human that can see me, the real me, on any other day than Halloween. You will give me many babes."

It's as if I can see steam coming from her ears. She is livid. "I don't believe in prophecies or demons or any of this. And my job contract said nothing about being a broodmare for the CEO. I read it very carefully."

Her words are sassy, but her eyes flash with something else. Fear, perhaps, at the truth she cannot yet accept. It matters not. She will come to embrace her destiny, as I have embraced mine.

Tonight she will be mine in body and soul, and by the time I am finished, she will be ripe with my child. The prophecy will be fulfilled. My curse will be broken. I will no longer be alone.

I circle her like a predator corralling its prey. Her fear is an aphrodisiac, spurring the demon within. My eyes glow, magic crackling at my fingertips.

"You cannot escape your fate, little angel. Tonight you will be filled with my seed."

"You're not the boss of me." Her breath hitches. "Okay, I mean, you're not the boss of me outside the office where you are literally the boss of me. And now I'm babbling. Because this is what I do when I am nervous and you are making me very, very nervous." She inhales a deep breath. "Besides, you told me that what happened between us on Halloween couldn't be repeated, remember?"

"I thought you were my employee a few minutes ago."

"I *am* your employee," she protests.

"Well, now you are no longer my employee."

"You're firing me?"

"I'm *breeding* you."

Maribelle shrieks, attempting to dart around me. I seize her by the waist and bring her against my chest.

"I do love a good chase. We can play games later. But now we must talk, as you humans do love to talk. We shall get it over with so we can get onto better things."

She shoves away from me and I allow it. This time.

"This is insane, Lucrael. No, *Mr. Blackstone*." As if saying my last name will return us to simple boss and employee. "We had a one-night stand. An encounter you fled from while I slept, let me remind you."

Ah. Her pride is wounded. "I'm sorry if I hurt your feelings, angel. Humans can see my demon attributes on Halloween, when the veil is the thinnest, but it's safe to roam because everyone is in costume. However, I needed to be away from humanity before dawn when the change came again. The change happens in ripples, not all at once. It would be hard to explain why my horns were blinking in and out of focus."

"And glowing eyes."

I nod. "Yes."

"And teeth. My goodness, and your tongue." She blushes.

She did so enjoy my tongue that night. And my tongue enjoyed her as well.

"That is something I can control, actually."

I open my mouth and let my tongue reshape and show her what she had stuffed in her sweet cunt the other night. I cannot wait to get her back on it. The memory of her quaking thighs as she came on my tongue has haunted me since Halloween. I need to taste her again, to make her come and come until she's a writhing mess, begging me to take her.

Tonight she will be mine. There is no other option.

I wiggle the tips and she gasps, turning a fetching shade of pink. "I knew it was forked! I thought I had to be imagining it."

I bring my tongue back in, returning it to a human shape.

"You loved having my tongue in your pussy. You came all over my face, naughty girl." I pause to adjust my pants. "I was so hard for you, Maribelle. So hard I nearly exploded when you squeezed my head between your thighs and stroked my horns. I wanted to plunge my cock inside your sweet, wet pussy and fill you with my seed." I let my words sink in and her blush deepens. "But I couldn't."

"Why not?" she whispers.

"My true cock is visible on Halloween as well."

She shakes her head. "I don't understand. What does that mean?"

I pull her back into my body so she can feel the bulge in my pants that shames any human male she has ever seen. "I could not explain away my demon cock as part of a costume. It's not human. It's better."

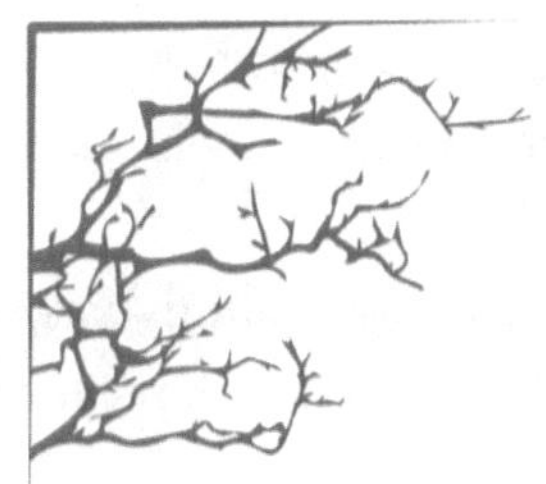

Five
Lucrael

Maribelle tries to put distance between us, but I push against her center so she can feel every inch of my beastly member through our clothes.

"It's way too big."

There is that sweet scent of fear again. "It's exactly what you need. What you deserve. It will keep you full and satisfied." I pull back enough to place her hand on my erection. "I'll give you the best orgasm you have ever dreamed of having."

"Better than the other night?"

"Better than the other night." How intoxicating to know that I've already given her the best orgasm of her life. "And then you'll beg for another and another. And I'll give them to you. Until you are swollen and heavy with my young."

"This is insane," she breathes, though she squeezes my cock gently as if unable to stop herself. A look of wonder softens her features briefly.

Then she lets go of it and her emotions whiplash, her hands going to her hips. "You didn't leave me your cell number. You say you had to leave before dawn, but you weren't interested in me contacting you, so I'm not convinced that you suddenly want me to bear your demon offspring."

The monster inside me is getting impatient. It's not her fault, and I must remember that she has been treated poorly by human men.

I'm not used to answering to another. In all my dealings with humans, I always have the upper hand. Not one person has ever questioned my motives or argued their point.

Until now.

Maribelle doesn't show the natural deference to me that her kind normally does by instinct. She does not lower her eyes first. She does not show a healthy fear of a predator in her midst.

Instead, she challenges me. *Me.*

It would be a lie to say I do not enjoy her little rebellion. However, my inner beast rages, wanting to show my dominance. I take one large step forward, and she takes a step back. I move closer, she moves away. I keep up the game until her back is pushed against the wall and I have her cornered.

"You will obey me. You will bear my young. You will do as I say and you will not question me. Do you understand?"

She looks up at me with...well it certainly isn't deference. "I most certainly will *not.*"

I swallow the roar threatening to sound. "I sent you flowers this morning, Maribelle. They'll be delivered to your apartment sometime this afternoon, though you will not be there because you will be here, in my bed, screaming my name."

I didn't even have Evelyn arrange it, which is good since she would have thought it strange I was sending her new assistant flowers. "I stopped at the florist myself to pick them out because I wanted to hand write the card. I had every intention of contacting you again. I did not know I would see you in my office today first."

It's amazing how mercurial human emotions are. She loses her glare, softens, then her features firm up again...all in the space of a breath. "And the card says?"

I pinch the bridge of my nose. I spent all day yesterday trying to form the right message. I'm still not convinced I accomplished it well. "*The demon misses his angel.* And my personal number below it."

She thinks about this for a moment. She wants to believe me. She wants to know she was special even before I knew she was the one. "I've never had a one-night stand before," she says, her voice quiet and vulnerable.

"I am aware."

"I didn't like it."

I raise my eyebrow because I know for a fact she liked it very, very much.

An exaggerated eye roll from her follows. "I mean I didn't like the feeling of waking up alone. I didn't like being intimate with a stranger and having him disappear like it never happened."

"You will never wake up alone again."

She gasps. "You're outrageous. You're going too fast."

"Am I? You are my *bride*, Maribelle. Cease this arguing so I may please you with my cock."

She wheezes in a breath. "Have you ever heard of dating? It usually happens before brides and babies. What if I don't *want* to be your bride?"

"I can smell your arousal. You cannot hide your feelings from me."

Her eyes shoot daggers at me, my little spitfire. This lifetime with her will be even more fun than anticipated. "Being attracted to you is different from wanting to *marry* you and procreate. I'm an old-fashioned girl. I want a marriage based on love."

I loosen my hold on her, surprised by a human for the first time in many years. "You do not think you can love me, Maribelle?"

She withdraws a bit. "I do not think you can love me, Lucrael," she says softly.

The heart I didn't know I possess breaks at her words. "I have searched the world for you for over three hundred years. We are fated."

The defeat on her features is something I must find a way to erase. "That's not love. Even if I can wrap my mind around 'fated' mates, that doesn't mean it's love. That's almost like duty. A reflex. I want something deeper than that. We don't even know each other."

Humans throughout history seem to live to make things more difficult than they are. I am smart enough not to say that to her, of course.

I lead her to the couch. "To be fated is so much more than mere love." Maribelle balks, but I sit and settle her onto my lap. "I have waited centuries for you. Please at least allow me to try to show you. We can get to know each other as we go."

"What if you change your mind? What if you decide you want someone new? That maybe having a prophesied ball-and-chain doesn't suit you after being a bachelor for centuries. What happens to me then?"

I grow very still, aware that she is used to "men" like the one I met at the bar. The one who hurt her. But it tries my patience to have to explain something so elemental. "Once I have claimed you, it would be easier to pull out my still-beating heart than abandon you."

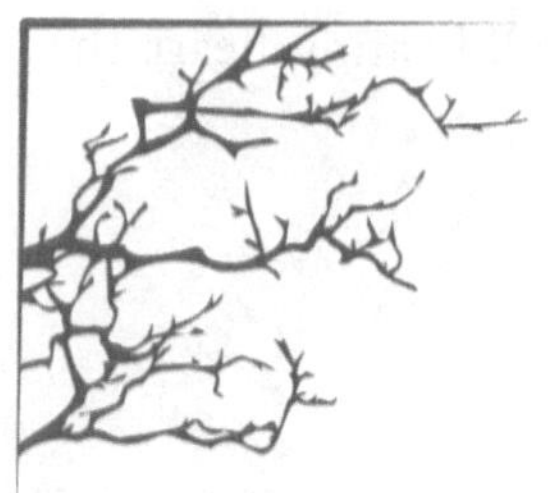

Six
Lucrael

The wheels turn in her mind, mulling over every angle. "You understand that in my world, a demon is an evil monster from legends. That for me to accept that you are a demon and that I am to be your bride or whatever means that I have to completely let go of everything I know to be true. I have to believe in the supernatural and the impossible."

"Yes, that is true. Your kind has erased the supernatural from their belief system, but that does not mean we ceased to exist."

"And you are saying that even though you don't know anything about me, you believe that I am your fated mate. And that living without me after claiming me will cause you pain."

"Anguish, yes."

"And that I should just accept this all to be true. That you will be faithful and adoring and not eat me during a full moon."

"I intend to eat you as often as I can get your panties off of you."

She pushes at me. "I'm serious."

"Yes, I understand." I stroke her cheek softly. "But if I am to prove myself to you, it will take more than just words. I will need to show you the depths of the feelings we will share together. You're not just my fated mate. I'm yours as well. The other half of your soul. Not all humans get one of those."

The shock of that has her eyes widening. I can feel her pulse quickening as she processes this new information. She leans into my embrace, her body melting into mine.

"I want to believe you," she whispers. "So demons are real. I guess I have to accept that." Her heart is softening to me already. I can see it in her eyes. "Are you like a minion of Satan or anything?"

She's not ready to hear that Satan doesn't exist and is a construct of human religion used to control the masses, and it's not something I want to debate with her about right now anyway.

"I'm not evil, but I can be a monster. I've learned to temper that, but it's still there. I'm arrogant–"

"Oh, I know." There. In her eyes, a little sparkle flashes when she teases me.

"I will let your taunt go this time. Do not make a habit of it."

She bites her lip. Not in fear. She is trying not to laugh.

At *me*. I choose to allow that this time.

"I am dominant, used to my own way. I can rend the limbs from a man without breaking a sweat, but I have not done so for a very long time." Her eyes narrow, questioning me silently. "At least one hundred years. Maybe two."

"Are you teasing me?"

"No." She doesn't reply so I continue, "I like to hunt game, but do not require a weapon for the kill. I will occasionally disappear for a day or two to hunt, but you need not concern yourself for my safety."

"I wouldn't dream of it."

I choose to let her sarcasm go.

"Forest creatures recognize me as a predator instinctively. Most humans do as well, though I don't hunt them. Any more."

The frown on her face is adorable. I can tell she is trying to put the pieces together in her mind. "So you are not evil, but you have done evil?"

I nod. Technically, yes. But some of them really deserved it. "I am not the same man I was even a hundred years ago. I have learned to control my temper and my darker urges. I will never be completely tamed, but I can be trusted to protect you."

She nods. "Okay, what else?"

"You'll be happy to know that I cannot be summoned by rituals, satanic or otherwise."

"Oh, that is good to know." Her humor is returning and I may be sorry for it.

"I am a primal being that has been domesticated, more or less, by centuries of living side by side with humans. But those who cross me wish they hadn't. I can be ruthless."

She is quiet for a long while. "Tell me more about this cock that is so much better than a human cock."

The weight of the world lifts off my chest. She is willing to try. And she said *cock*. I want to hear her say that word again and again.

"My cock is going to scare you. You are going to say it's too big. You'll say it hurts. But you will take all of it in your pussy because you will need to feel it so badly. Because you were made to take my cock. No other woman has seen its true form. Just you. It is only for you." Her breath hitches, but she doesn't interrupt. "When you take me, you will be so full and stretched, and you will come so hard that you won't even think about saying it hurts, even if it does a little." Her mouth opens in a silent *oh*. "Then I will allow you my seed. You will feel my cock twitch inside you for days."

"Oh," she breathes it aloud this time. Her eyes are wide and her mouth is hanging open.

"Demon cum is addicting, angel. You're going to want it in you every day. It will make you feel so fucking good. Once I let you suck it from me, you will become a nuisance, always trying to get my pants off me. The taste of it will be your favorite flavor."

"Oh," she whispers again. "Are you for real right now?"

"But you will not drink from my cock until you are pregnant. We will waste no seed until there is a baby in your belly. I will, however, let you clean our combined cum from my cock after lovemaking."

"How romantic." Her voice is dripping with sarcasm.

I chuckle. "Wait until you have tried it. You will beg for more. You will crave it, and if licking it off of me after we have fucked is the only way you can get some of it in your mouth, you'll beg to do it."

"Remember how you said you were arrogant?"

"Are you going to pretend you don't like my arrogance?"

She sighs. "I've never met anyone like you. And I've never felt..."

"The instant connection? The loneliness after we parted? I've never felt it before either, and I've been around a lot longer than you. Are you ready to finish what we started on Halloween?"

"I think, yes. Yes I am. Show it to me, Lucrael. Show me this magical demon cock, and I'll let you know if it lives up to the hype."

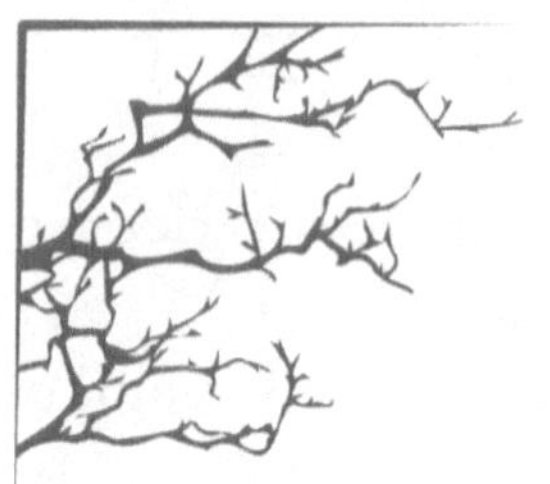

Seven
Maribelle

Lucrael sweeps me up and we are magically transported into his bedroom.

So this is a demon lair. It's all very dark and masculine. A little on the goth side compared to the rest of the penthouse. His large bed was made for sex, with dark satin sheets and soft pillows piled high. My eyes scan the room and stop on something gold and sparkly on his nightstand that doesn't match the vibe.

"Is that my halo? Did you take the halo from my angel costume home with you the other night?" And put it in a place of prominence in his bedroom?

The way he tenderly looks at the halo like it's precious makes butterflies take flight in my stomach. "Guilty," he responds, his deep voice so irresistible.

Knowing that he couldn't bear to part with something from our Halloween tryst helps me believe that he's been telling me the truth. That I am special to him. That he wanted me that night and wants me now even before he knew I could see his true form. That I was his mate.

Being desired for myself is a powerful aphrodisiac.

I unbutton my shirt while staring into his eyes. He watches me undress as I drop my blouse to the floor. My eyes are not able

to break away from his gaze as I unlatch my bra and let the girls
out.

He grabs my ass and pulls me against his hard body. I love
the way his muscles feel under my fingertips.

He reaches down to squeeze my breast. "So beautiful. So
perfect." He slowly draws a circle around my nipple with his
finger. "When you are demon seeded, these breasts will grow full
and heavy with milk."

Yes, demon seeded. That sounds so fucking dirty.

I want to feel his skin against mine, so I reach for his shirt.
My hands are shaking as I unbutton it and push it off his
shoulders. I run my hands over his hard chest, his eight-pack, and
his broad shoulders.

Lucrael is a work of art.

He reaches for my skirt and unzips it, then pushes it down to
the floor. I step out of my shoes and step out of my skirt.

He grinds his erection against me, and I'm dying of curiosity.
"Can I see it now?"

"Patience." Lucrael's hot breath tickles my ear as he whispers,
"I will fill you with my seed tonight, again and again, until it
takes root inside your womb."

A delicious shiver races through me. I clench my thighs
together, acutely aware of the slick heat gathering between them.

I accused him of having a breeding fetish, but maybe it's me.

"You will carry my young," he rasps, one hand sliding down
to rest on my lower belly in a possessive claim. "Your body ripe
and swollen with the fruit of our lovemaking. I will worship you
in every way. You will want for nothing as your body carries and
nourishes my demon seed."

I gasp, trembling at the images flooding my mind. Of my belly rounding, my breasts swelling with milk. Of Lucrael lavishing affection on me, tending to my every need as I carry his child.

Okay, I definitely have a breeding kink too.

"Yes," I breathe, arching into his touch. Just like the other night, nothing matters but this connection between us. "I want that. I want everything with you."

A low rumble of approval vibrates through his chest. "You shall have it. I will make you mine in every way."

His hand drifts lower, fingers teasing at my slick entrance beneath my underwear. I'm primed and ready, pulsing with need for his claiming.

Lucrael chuckles, a darkly sinful sound. "So wet for me already. You ache to be filled, don't you?"

"Yes," I whimper, beyond shame. "Show it to me," I whisper. "I want to see it. I want to see your demon cock."

I'm not sure who the person speaking with my voice is. I think I've said the word cock ten times in my entire life before today. Now I guess I'm ravenous for it.

Lucrael undoes his pants and pulls them down with his boxer briefs, allowing me my first look at the promised weapon between his legs.

Weapon indeed.

Unlike a human's, Lucrael's large phallus is textured with a raised, braided ridge that twists around it from just below his cock head all the way to the base.

Then there are the spikes.

Jutting from his body in a ring around the base of his impressive girth are spikes of inky black. I'm not sure why I didn't expect a demon cock to look like some kind of hardcore BDSM implement of torture, but I'm afraid I've made a grave error.

All the blood leaves my face and spots appear in my vision.

"They won't hurt you," Lucrael assures me. "They are soft cleats designed to give you even more pleasure as we join."

"How?"

"Your clit is not the only sensitive part of your pussy, angel. The barbs will provide extra stimulation. They're not sharp."

I bite my lip, uncertain.

"Trust me," Lucrael says. "I will make it good for you. You will not regret taking me into you." He takes my hand and rubs one of the barbs. His abdomen tenses in pleasure at my touch. I'm relieved that the tip of the spike didn't break my skin.

The pleasure he obviously derived from my touch bolsters my confidence. I run my finger over the braided ridge and he shivers.

Ribbed for both our pleasure it would seem.

But the girth. My mouth goes dry. The girth of his giant demon cock is also troubling. "Will it fit? It doesn't look like it will fit."

Lucrael grins. "I assure you, it will fit. And you will love every minute of it."

The more I stare at it, the more heat blooms between my legs. The anticipation is overwhelming.

"Wait until you taste it, angel. Get on your knees."

I do, my mouth watering. He stands before me and I reach out to the object of my desire.

"Stick out your tongue," he commands me.

I obediently do as he commands, and he presses the heavy tip against my tongue. It's warmer than I thought and tastes of exotic spices, yet also sweet.

"Yes," he growls. "That's it. Taste me, angel. Taste my essence."

The sensation is indescribable as I lick and swirl my tongue around the head of Lucrael's cock, his precum bedazzling me.

"Put it in your mouth," he commands.

I'm pretty sure the tip is about all I can fit in my mouth, but I do as he says.

"Suck. Just a little."

I suck lightly, and the taste is amazing. I moan, stroking his cock with my hand.

I want it all. I want his cock to be a part of me, to fill every inch of me as he promised. I want to know what it's like to be claimed by Lucrael.

"Good girl," he murmurs. He rubs a hand down the nape of my neck. "You will make me spill too soon. My seed is for your sweet pussy this time."

The heavy scent of our arousal fills the room, and I can barely think straight. My body is a live wire, every nerve ending tingling as his smoldering gaze pins me in place like prey. His cock, so different from anything I've ever seen, beckons to me, promising ecstasy I never thought possible.

"Lucrael," I whimper, my voice shaking with need. "I need you to breed me now."

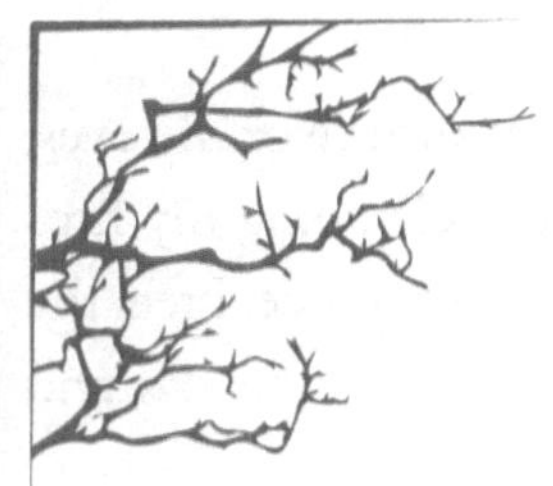

Eight
Maribelle

"**I**s that what you want, Maribelle?" he purrs, his voice low and dangerous. "You want me to claim you, make you mine forever?"

My heart thuds wildly, the words spilling from my lips before I can even think. "Yes."

"Very well, my love," he murmurs, his eyes glinting with something akin to triumph, though not unkind. "I'll give you what you crave."

He pulls me to my feet and rips my underwear off my body. His fingers find their way to my waist, gripping tightly as he pulls me flush against him. The sensation of his powerful arms encircling me sends a thrill coursing through my veins, and I can feel the outline of his massive cock pressing against my stomach.

He picks me up in his strong arms and tosses me gently on the bed, following me as I bounce lightly.

"You're mine," he growls. "Take a deep breath," he whispers into my ear. "I'll guide you through this."

"Okay," I reply shakily, my anticipation heightening in response to his confident tone. My heart races as he positions me just the way he wants me. His touch sends tingles radiating throughout my body, each sensation heightened by our connection.

"You are so wet. Are you ready?"

I nod, unable to speak as I gaze into his otherworldly eyes, filled with a mix of tenderness and ferocity. Gripping my hips firmly in his hands, he positions himself at my entrance. I feel the tip of his monstrous cock pressing against me, its unique size and shape intimidating yet exhilarating.

"Oh shit," I say. That thing is big.

"Remember to breathe, Maribelle," Lucrael says softly, his breath hot against my ear. I release a shaky breath and try to relax, focusing on the moment and the connection between us.

He pushes forward, penetrating me with a slow, deliberate force. The pressure is immense, unlike anything I've ever experienced before. My body stretches to accommodate him, but my spine tenses.

"Easy now," he coaxes, pausing for a moment before continuing his steady advance. "You need to relax." His length slides further inside me, filling me, the pressure almost too much to bear. I bite my lip, trying to hold back a moan, but the sound escapes me anyway.

He begins moving within me, each thrust causing waves of pleasure to crash through me.

"Lucrael," I pant, the sensations building inside me making coherent thought nearly impossible. I grip onto him, feeling the power within him even as he moves with such care and control. "Please... more."

"As you wish."

He picks up the pace, his thrusts growing more forceful and insistent. The braided texture of his cock rubbing against my inner walls is almost too much, the friction becoming more intense with each movement. Nothing has ever felt this good before. I don't actually think I am supposed to feel this good.

"I'm almost all the way in."

My breath halts. "Almost?"

That can't be true. There's no room for any more of him. What the hell?

He chuckles. "Remember those soft barbs at the base, my angel. They are going to make you fly."

I gasp as he pushes further, every inch a new sensation. Every ridge and ripple of his cock inside me gives off little sparks. My body is stretched and filled in a way that should not be pleasurable. Yet, somehow, pleasure is all I know.

I am building toward a really big orgasm, but I feel like I'm having little ones with every thrust now. Appetizer orgasms. Appegasms.

Then I feel the barbs. The spikes are not sharp, but they add an extra layer of pleasure as he moves, massaging the sensitive flesh around my clit.

He quickens his pace, his thrusts becoming more urgent. I grab his horns, instinctively pulling him into me. He groans, the sound low and masculine, as he pushes into me. The sensation is overwhelming, and I know I'm close to coming.

Lucrael growls in approval, picking up speed, his hips bucking as he fills me. "So eager now, aren't you? Such a good defiled angel you are."

His words send a rush of heat straight to my core. Yes, defiled. Yes, absolutely. "More, tell me more."

"Oh my little darling slut. You're a slave to my cock now, aren't you? You want to be used by your demon, don't you?"

"Yes." I clench around his pistoning length, spiraling higher with each expert thrust.

"Do you want my cum?"

"Put a baby in me," I plead, my body quivering with need.

Lucrael's eyes glow, pupils dilating until only a thin rim of crimson remains. "Look at me," he commands, voice dropping an octave.

I stare up at him, transfixed by the inferno blazing behind his gaze. His hips snap forward in a punishing rhythm, cock spearing into my slick channel again and again. The pleasure-pain is exquisite, shredding my senses until I can only feel, only want.

A familiar pressure builds at the base of my spine, molten pleasure coiling tight. I'm so close, hovering at the edge of bliss.

"Come for me," he demands. "Come all over this cock, my filthy angel."

My entire body clenches, my muscles straining as the tension in my core reaches a breaking point. The orgasm roars through me, my vision exploding into a million golden sparks. Waves of ecstasy flow from my core, showering my body in pleasure.

He keeps moving inside me, his cock sliding in and out, prolonging my orgasm until I feel like I'm drifting in a sea of bliss. "So beautiful," he whispers. "The way you come on my cock is the most beautiful thing I have ever seen."

His voice is like warm honey, thick and sweet. I shiver, his name on my lips a reverent whisper. "Lucrael."

I moan as he increases his pace, driving me toward another orgasm. He keeps me riding the high, my body responding to every expert thrust of his hips. I'm not sure I've actually stopped coming since we began. My orgasm just keeps changing in intensity.

Lucrael growls, his thrusts growing more insistent and forceful. I can feel him fighting to hold back, but now I want him to let go. I want to feel him come. I want him to lose control because of me.

"Lucrael," I whisper, gripping his horns. "Please."

His eyes blaze, the intensity of his gaze like another physical touch that singes me. The muscles in his arms and legs tense. He stops moving, still buried deep within me. His cock swells and pulses deep within my core. He groans, his body tensing as he finally, finally comes.

White-hot pleasure washes over me, Lucrael's essence filling me. The pleasure seems to intensify, each pump of his cock sending another wave of heat through me. I reach for his rock-hard ass and pull him closer. As if he might pull out too soon and deprive me of even one drop of my new obsession.

His cock is still thick and hard inside me, rubbing against my walls. "Come for me," he murmurs. "I can feel you clenching around me, my angel. Come for me one more time."

I grip his horns tighter, shuddering as another orgasm builds deep in my core.

I think I might die from it.

Lucrael is still coming. I can feel the pulses of his cock, filling me again and again and again.

He groans, his hips snapping forward in a deep thrust, his cock pulsing one last time. If I do manage to live through this ecstasy, I can't guarantee I'll leave this bed willingly.

"I claim you. You're mine now," he rasps. "Mine to breed, mine to keep."

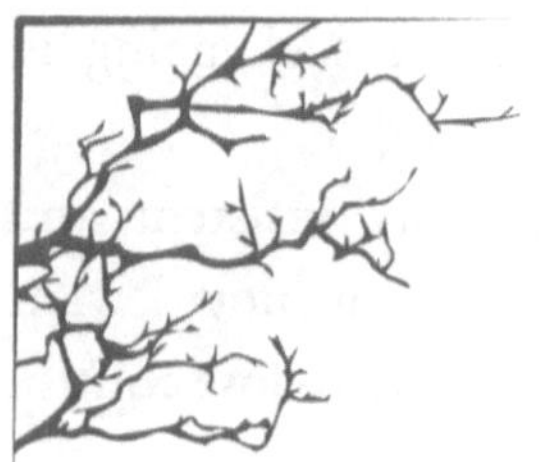

Nine
Maribelle

I peel back the foil on the Thanksgiving turkey and inhale the savory scent of rosemary and thyme. My mouth waters.

I'm pleased with our efforts. I had no idea on Halloween that I would spend Thanksgiving Day making a feast side by side with a demon.

"Look at that bird, plump and golden brown," Luc says, coming up behind me. His hands grip my waist, pulling me against his hard body. I lean into him, relishing the warmth radiating off his chest.

"Perfectly cooked, I'd say." I turn my head to nuzzle his neck, breathing in the familiar scent of sandalwood soap and something uniquely Luc. "Mmm, smells delicious."

His lips brush the curve of my neck and a delicious shiver in my body makes me wiggle my toes. "You're wet. I can smell you. Let me make you come."

"The guests will be here any minute," I protest halfheartedly. My body betrays me, arching into his touch. I can feel the bulge in his trousers pressing against my backside and I want it.

Will I ever stop wanting it every minute of the day?

"We have time." His hands slide under my shirt, fingers teasing my nipples into hardened peaks.

I'm going to combust right here in this kitchen. I bite my lip to stifle a moan.

The doorbell rings, shattering the moment.

I pull away with an exaggerated sigh. "Saved by the bell."

Luc growls, eyes gleaming. "This isn't over. I'll have you for dessert."

"Maybe I'll have *you* for dessert."

He grins, a devilish gleam in his eye. "I look forward to it."

If only. He teases me with a dessert he won't let me have yet.

Lucrael insists on finishing inside my pussy and never in my mouth. He's so delicious that it's unfair. He will eat me for hours, but won't come in my mouth.

I often clean his cock after we make love. But even that isn't enough. I want more. I want all of him. I want to feel him twitch and shudder as he comes in my mouth.

I straighten my clothes and hurry to answer the door, holding the backs of my hands to my flushed cheeks. I throw open the door.

"Gia!" I hug her. "Happy Thanksgiving."

Only one of my girl gang is joining us as my other friends have local family. Gia and I have traditionally spent the holidays together since college.

She looks around Luc's penthouse, the first time she's seen it. "Wow. It's beautiful. I know you told me it was, but seeing it in person is something else."

Luc joins us and is charming as usual. Gia has been his number one fan since Halloween when he pretended to be my boyfriend to make Mark jealous. She liked him more when she saw how well he treats me. Like I'm his queen.

Which he tells me I am.

It's hard for me to believe that Gia can't see his horns, though. Like...they are *right* there. How can I be the only one who notices them?

"You look happy," Gia tells me. "I don't think I've ever seen you this happy."

I smile and glance at Luc. He's watching me with a knowing look in his eyes.

"We are," I reply.

Luc takes my hand and brings it to his lips. "Very happy indeed."

"You said your boss, Ms. James, is coming too?" Gia asks, taking a glass of wine from Luc as we sit in the living room.

I pass on the wine and get a look from both of them. I thought I'd be able to keep my suspicions to myself a little longer. I don't want to get Lucrael's hopes up until I know for sure.

When Gia asked me in the beginning if I was being careful with Luc, I answered that I was. I am careful. I have to be careful or that demon cock would tear me up. That's not what she meant, and I know it. But I couldn't tell her that I'm letting my brand-new boyfriend try to knock me up as often as possible. I can't tell her that the idea of getting pregnant with a "man" I've known for less than a month turns me on so much I'm willing to not be logical or smart.

Just like I can't tell her that he's my fated mate or that he's a demon. These are things I can only talk about with Lucrael.

"My *ex*-boss is coming, yes," I answer Gia. "Evelyn is Luc's assistant, but I only got to work with her for one day as her assistant." I glance at Luc. "The CEO here has a strict workplace romance policy."

Gia laughs. "Now you have a sugar daddy. That sounds like more fun anyway."

"A sugar daddy. I guess I do. It wasn't my intention. Luc likes to spoil me."

Luc kisses the top of my head. "I waited a long time to find my angel. I'm a little possessive of her time."

A little? I want to ask. He had me moved into the penthouse less than a week after we met. I wanted to keep working, kind of. But if he's not at the office, he's inside my body. There's not a lot of time for another job when my full time job seems to be getting pregnant.

And I'll want to stay home with our child when it happens anyway. Going back to school is an option Luc has floated past me, and I might do that. Getting my master's degree was a dream I never thought I could afford.

Evelyn arrives, bringing pies. Since Luc is the son she never had, he usually went to her home for Thanksgiving. But this is the first holiday she's spent as a widow, so we offered to host this year.

You know...because demons are known for holiday entertaining.

I think he only ever went to her house because it was easier than trying to explain why he didn't want to. He thinks human holidays are odd. Since his children will be half-human, and their mother loves holidays, he'll just need to get over himself.

Evelyn does watch me carefully through dinner. She worries that I'm a gold digger, probably. I mean, I worked for half a day before leaving with the CEO, never to return.

Our small dinner party is a success, the food disappearing amid lively conversation and second helpings for all. I glance at Luc, catching his heated gaze from across the table. A secret smile passes between us, the memory of our interrupted tryst simmering below the surface. The night is still young.

The guests finally bid their farewells, lingering in the foyer to exchange hugs and wish us a happy Thanksgiving. I close the door behind them with a contented sigh, leaning back against the cool wood.

Luc is there in an instant, pinning me in place with his body. "Alone at last." His lips find my neck, teasing the sensitive skin with teeth and tongue, gorging on me.

I gasp, tilting my head to give him better access. Then he nips me with those fangs. "You weren't kidding about me being dessert."

"Never." He lifts me easily, my legs wrapping around his waist as he carries me into the living room. The city glimmers below us, a sea of lights stretching endlessly into the distance.

Luc presses me against the glass, the chill seeping through my clothes. I shiver as his hands slide under my skirt, questing fingers finding my center. "So wet already," he murmurs against my throat. "You've been thinking about this all through dinner, haven't you?"

I moan in response, beyond words as he strokes me slowly. The coil of pleasure winds tighter and tighter within me until I'm trembling on the edge of release. Just a little more...

A diamond catches the light as Luc holds up his other hand, a stunning solitaire ring nestled in the black velvet box. My breath catches in my throat.

"Marry me."

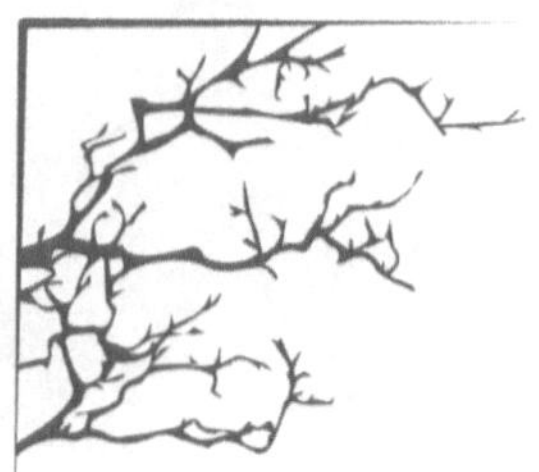

Ten
Maribelle

It's not a question, of course. Lucrael doesn't ever ask for permission. An apex predator problem.

"It's too soon," I say.

His demon eyes gleam brighter than any jewel. "It's not. Marry me."

"For someone who claims to think human customs are a silly waste of time—"

Our lips meet in a searing kiss as he places the ring on my finger. "Marry me," he repeats.

The city glimmers below the penthouse windows, a sea of lights stretching endlessly into the night. In this moment, all the world seems to fade away until only Luc and I remain.

I guess it's a little silly that I've been actively trying to get pregnant for weeks, but think it's too soon to get married. "Yes," I say. "I'll marry you."

Luc's lips find my neck, teasing a slow path up to my ear. "You're mine now, little angel," he rasps, littering the floor with our clothes.

Luc lifts me, pinning me against the penthouse window. "Look at them," Luc whispers, nodding at the city below. "So blissfully unaware. If only they knew what was happening right above their heads." His eyes gleam with mischief and longing.

"I wish they could see us," I say, reaching my hand around his cock. "I want everyone to know I'm yours. To see how this huge demon cock fills me up and makes me scream."

Luc's eyes flash with pleasure. "And I want them to see how I make you come. How your tight little human pussy milks me dry. Let them watch me breed my little human."

As he slides deep inside me, I close my eyes and revel in the sensation. I know they can't see us, but I imagine the whole city watching as Luc brings me to the edge of ecstasy. His thrusts become faster and faster, pushing me closer and closer to the edge.

"I will fill you soon. Are you ready for my cum?" he whispers.

I moan in response, my insides trembling with anticipation. "I crave your cum, Lucrael. I want it inside me all the time."

Luc's eyes blaze with a feral hunger, and he pumps into me harder and faster. "When you are round with my child, you will drink the cum from my cock. I will fill your throat with it until you are overflowing, my naughty angel."

My walls clamp down around him, milking and begging for more. His cock swells inside me as I come. With one final thrust, he spills his hot cum deep, so deep.

We lower to the floor, sated for now. My head rests on Luc's chest, rising and falling with each of his breaths.

"In all my years, I have known no other like you, Maribelle. I promise to cherish you for the rest of your days."

"Our days, demon."

His eyes are solemn, gaze distant. "Immortality to walk this Earth alone is my curse. I'm afraid you will one day go where I cannot follow."

I try to picture Luc unchanged while I grow old and wither away. Panic claws at my chest, and I scramble to sit up.

"I'm going to die," I whisper. "You're going to watch me die."

"Yes," he says sadly.

"You told me that losing a fated mate is like tearing out a still-beating heart."

"Yes," he repeats.

"So you will mourn me forever? How is that fair? Why did you look for your human mate for so long when you knew that after you found me and lost me, you'd be worse off than before?"

Tears spill down my cheeks as I look at the man who has become my whole world. How could I ever leave him? How can I condemn him to an eternity of grief and loneliness?

"And our children?" I ask. "Will they be immortal like you? Or will they be human like me?"

"I don't know. The prophecy was vague on those kinds of details."

A sob catches in my throat. Tonight was supposed to be a celebration of new beginnings, but instead, I glimpse the ending waiting for us at the end of this road.

Luc holds me close, his arms wrapped around me like iron bands. I listen to the steady beat of his heart, a rhythm as ageless as time itself.

After a long moment, I ask in a hushed tone. "Is there a way?"

"What do you mean?"

"Can you make me like you? Bite me or something?" I ask. Though he's done that countless times already. Marking me as his, he says. "Can you make me immortal, so we could be together forever without fear of death coming between us?"

An eternity is a long time, long enough to grow weary of life and long for an end that will never come. It's not something I even think I want for myself.

"I'm not a vampire," he answers.

"Are vampires real too?"

He chuckles. "You do not want to meet one. Trust me."

"I don't want you to mope around for eternity, either." I sigh. I don't want to waste any more of our time together with secrets. "I'm late."

"Late for what? I thought you told me you don't participate in the late-night Black Friday traditions."

"I don't. My period is late."

Lucrael goes still then pulls me impossibly closer. "I suspected when you didn't take the wine at dinner. How do you feel?"

"Cautiously optimistic? I don't want to get too far ahead of myself. I was going to wait to tell you until I was sure."

He kisses my forehead and pulls me into his lap, cradling me in his arms. "I've spent centuries mourning a future that would never be. Yet, here you are."

"I might not be pregnant. I'm just a couple days late."

"Then let's try again, just in case."

"You can't be ready yet..."

Lucrael puts my hand on his already hard cock. "I assure you I can." He moves out from under me. "Perhaps I should get you ready, angel."

Out comes his tongue, forked and stronger and thicker than a human's tongue. And my demon knows how to use it.

"I am going to make you scream." His voice is thick and deep. "And then I am going to do it again and again until you blackout. Your pussy is about to be possessed by a demon."

I am already wet, dripping with anticipation. Luc's eyes are the glint of a shark, and I am his prey. He licks his lips in anticipation of a feast.

I lie back, spreading my legs to give him better access. Lucrael's tongue swipes up my folds, and my back arches in response. He growls, the vibration sending a shiver through me. He loves knowing how he affects me.

My hands fly to his horns, stroking each like a cock. He shudders and moans as I massage them. His horns are not as sensitive as his penis, but since I am the only one who can see them, being touched there is very erotic for him. Almost taboo.

As his tongue goes deeper, he finds that magic spot deep inside me. Then the forked tips wiggle, and I'm lost to an orgasm that's ripped out of me almost violently.

"That's one," he says against my mound. Then he goes in for two.

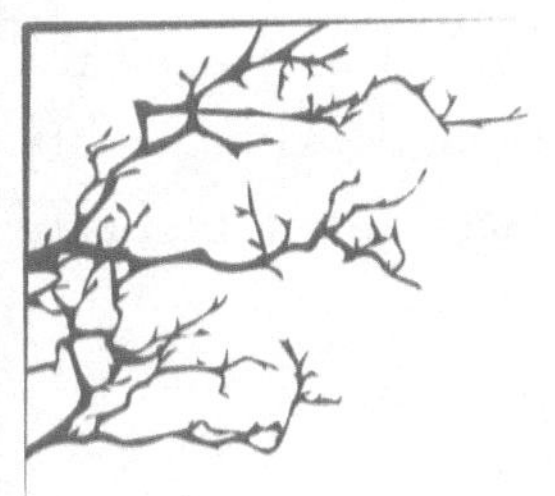

Epilogue
Lucrael

alloween, one year later
Spider webs drape across the entrance of the bar and orange lights cast a lurid glow over the revelers within. They don't know the veil is thin. They don't know real monsters revel among them on the only night they can appear in their true form.

Humans are simple creatures at times, choosing to ignore the supernatural world that exists in the shadows. But for those who know, Halloween is a night of excitement and danger. And for me, a demon, it's the perfect opportunity to indulge in my desires in the light.

I slip through the crowd, my eyes scanning for a suitable partner. I spot a voluptuous woman in a devil costume, her horns and tail accentuating her curves. She's perfect. I make my way towards her, my prey in my sights. Our eyes meet across the room and a smile curves her crimson lips.

She is exactly what I need tonight. As I get closer, I can see the way her dress clings to her curves, showing off her ample cleavage.

Perfect. The beast inside is awoken and I can feel my hunger rising.

I reach her and greet her with a wicked grin, playing the charming stranger as I do so well. She responds with a sultry smile, and I know that she's just as eager for a night of debauchery as I am.

"Looking for a little sin tonight?" she purrs.

"What sort of sin did you have in mind?"

"I was thinking something...wicked." She traces one sharp nail down my chest, her touch like fire even through the fabric. "Interested?"

A flash of heat races through my veins at the thought. All through the bar, lust and desire mingle with the scents of alcohol and sweat. A night for sin indeed, in more ways than one.

I grasp her chin, forcing her to meet my gaze. "Wife, you have no idea how wicked I can be." The words rumble in my chest, a promise of dark delights to come.

Tonight I will sate the beast and by dawn, this little devil will know the meaning of sin.

"Get a room," Gia complains from next to Maribelle.

Maribelle smiles and wraps her arms around my neck. "Hello, husband. I see you're wearing the same costume as last year."

"It worked didn't it? I snared you into my evil web with it."

Our infant daughter is home, snug in her crib. This is our first night out since she was born. Maribelle pumped before we left, but I notice she's not drinking. She must have decided she wanted to nurse tonight after all.

Much has changed for me—for us—since last Halloween. A year ago, the idea of a demon and a mortal woman walking into a bar together would have seemed like the setup to some twisted joke. But now, it's our reality, and one that I wouldn't trade for all the power in Hell.

"Hey, check that out." Gia points to a woman sitting in the corner, her long, flowing dress adorned with stars and moons, her head covered by an intricate veil. She is reading tarot cards for the curious patrons around her. Even from a distance, her presence exudes an aura of mystique.

It's not a costume. That right there is a very powerful witch. Her magic shimmers around her like a cloak, and I can feel the pull of it even from across the room. My curiosity is piqued, and I find myself drawn to her, eager to see what she can do.

Maribelle notices my interest and gives me a playful nudge. "Don't get any ideas, husband. You already have your hands full with me."

I chuckle and pull her closer. "I'm just curious, angel." I have to whisper the next part, "It's not every day you get to see a real witch in action."

As we approach, the witch looks up and meets my gaze. Her eyes are like pools of midnight, and I can feel the weight of her power in the air.

"Want to give it a try?" Maribelle grins. "See what the future holds?"

I already know what my future holds. The next few decades will be happy ones. And then my wife and children will die while I live on endlessly. I will have to eventually start a new identity and watch my descendants from afar as they live and die and still I carry on with this exhausting eternal life.

But I have now, and I refuse to taint my present with maudlin thoughts of the future.

"Welcome," she says, her voice smooth and enticing. "I've been waiting for you." The air around her seems to hum with energy.

We take our seats across from her in the booth. She has managed to create a bubble around us to drown out the sound of the busy club.

"I sense a powerful connection between the two of you," she says, studying our faces intently. Her fingers dance over the cards. "The fates have brought you together for a reason."

I exchange a knowing glance with Maribelle. The fates, indeed.

"Let's see what the cards have to say," the seer murmurs, drawing three cards from the deck and laying them out on the table.

Her deck is unlike the cards found in this realm. What the mortals around us cannot see is that the cards have an aura of their own and sparkle with magic.

She studies the first card. It depicts a figure cloaked in shadows, surrounded by images of transformation and renewal. "This card speaks of change and new beginnings. The choices you've made recently have set you on a path toward a different kind of life."

Maribelle squeezes my hand under the table, and I smile reassuringly at her.

She reveals the second card, depicting a passionate embrace between two figures, united in love and desire. "A strong bond connects you, one that transcends time and space. Your love will face challenges but will ultimately triumph over adversity."

The warmth of Maribelle's touch strengthens, and I tighten my grip on her hand, feeling the weight of the tarot reader's words settle heavily on my chest.

She turns over the last card. The image shows a figure breaking free from chains, illuminated by a radiant light. "This card represents hope and freedom. It signifies that you will find a way to break free from whatever binds you and embrace a life full of joy and love. A curse broken, perhaps. "

I feel a sudden rush of emotion, my chest swelling with a mixture of disbelief and hope. Could it be possible that there is a way for me to escape my ceaseless existence and live a mortal life with Maribelle?

"Tell me more of this broken curse," I demand.

The seer grabs my hand and traces something she sees on my palm. "You have a lifeline, demon."

"Impossible." I don't want to get my hopes up.

She shrugs. "Believe or believe not. Your palm tells a story."

Maribelle whispers, "I don't understand."

The fortune teller smiles kindly at her. "Immortals do not have lifelines on their palms. The demon you love is no longer immortal."

To live a mortal life with Maribelle, to grow old and die together. It would mean everything. "How can we know for sure?" I ask.

"There is only one way to test, and I do not recommend it because then you'd be dead. Perhaps you should just live each day as if it's your last, as it may very well be. And be more careful as you adjust to your new limitations."

I am *mortal*.

The realization sends a thrill of terror and joy twisting through me. How can I protect my family now, when any stray bullet or illness could end my life? But this gift is also profoundly precious. At last, I will share in the human experience of growing old together, of watching our daughter blossom and have children of her own.

"So you won't watch me wrinkle while you stay all hot and sexy?" Maribelle asks.

I laugh. "I will wrinkle at your side, I suppose."

"Whew." She squeezes my hand. "But are you okay with this?"

"My eternity begins and ends with you," I tell her, and seal my vow with a kiss.

Did you love *The Demon's Curvy Angel: A Halloween Romance*?
Then you should read *Bounced*[1] by Brill Harper!

Anvil is a rough, muscled bouncer working in a roadhouse. Sarah is a type-A, risk averse actuarial major with her whole life mapped out. She has a plan. Goals. And none of them include a tattooed, possessive bouncer.

She just wanted one night off from being perfect, boring, and careful. The night she steps out to try something out of her comfort zone, sneaking into a bar on the shady side of town, the alpha bouncer steps in to protect her from danger.Danger from everything but him.**Author's Confession: I don't even know**

---

1. https://books2read.com/u/mBMgLA

2. https://books2read.com/u/mBMgLA

if this could happen in real life. Luckily, it's a book. That means the hot, tatted, beardy bouncer can totally take one look at the virgin college student studying actuarial science and know he's going to marry the sh*t out of her. Right?

Anyway—totally safe romance-HEA, no cheating, hero wouldn't dream of looking at another woman after he sees Sarah. Trust Auntie Brill. It's a crazy story, but it's so much fun.

Read more at https://brillharper.com.

Also by Brill Harper

Blue Collar Bad Boys
Bounced
Nailed: A Blue Collar Bad Boys Book
Drilled: A Blue Collar Bad Boys Book
Wrecked: A Blue Collar Bad Boys Book
Laid: A Blue Collar Bad Boys Book
Tagged
Plowed
Bucked: A Blue Collar Bad Boys Book
Banged: A Blue Collar Bad Boys Book
Tapped: A Blue Collar Bad Boy Book

Dukes of Tempest
Mad Max
Dirty Dillon: A Small Town Age Gap Romance

Holiday Romance
The Demon's Curvy Angel: A Halloween Romance

It's Complicated
All Together
All at Once

Love in Brazen Bay
Wrong Number Text
The Right Stuff
So Wrong It's Right
Don't Get Me Wrong

Standalone
Dirty Jobs: a Blue Collar Bad Boys Collection
Notch on His Bedpost
Honeymoon With The Prince: A Royal Romance
Good Girl

Watch for more at https://brillharper.com.

About the Author

Unfailingly filthy...and super sweet

Brill's books are filthy/sweet for when you're in the mood for something a little over the top. Okay, a lot over the top. Sorry, not sorry. Members of the Brilliance Club get early access to all Brill's work and exclusive content not available anywhere else.

Find out more: **https://reamstories.com/brillharper**

Brill Harper is represented by Deidre Knight of The Knight Agency.

Read more at https://brillharper.com.